HISTORY OF INDIAN WITCHCRAFT AND STORY'S

INDIAN WITCHES ARE DOING CRAZY STUFF TO GET AHEAD IN THE MAGIC WORLD!

GOLU KUMAR

AF565475

Copyright © Golu Kumar
All Rights Reserved.

This book has been published with all efforts taken to make the material error-free after the consent of the author. However, the author and the publisher do not assume and hereby disclaim any liability to any party for any loss, damage, or disruption caused by errors or omissions, whether such errors or omissions result from negligence, accident, or any other cause.

While every effort has been made to avoid any mistake or omission, this publication is being sold on the condition and understanding that neither the author nor the publishers or printers would be liable in any manner to any person by reason of any mistake or omission in this publication or for any action taken or omitted to be taken or advice rendered or accepted on the basis of this work. For any defect in printing or binding the publishers will be liable only to replace the defective copy by another copy of this work then available.

Contents

ONE

The belief in witchcraft is very real to the present day among the Santals. All untimely deaths and illness which does not yield to treatment are attributed to the machinations of witches, and women are not unfrequently murdered in revenge for deaths that they are supposed to have caused or to prevent the continuance of illness for which they are believed to be responsible.

The Santal writer despite his education is a firm believer in witchcraft and details his own experiences. He has justification for his belief, for as was the case in Mediaeval Europe, women sometimes plead guilty to having caused death by witchcraft when there appears to be no adequate motive for a confession, which must involve them in the severest penalties.

Mr. Bodding is aware that Santal women do hold meetings at night at which mantras and songs are repeated, and at which they may believe they acquire uncanny powers; the exercise of such powers may also on occasion be assisted by the knowledge of vegetable poisons.

The witch may either herself cause death by 'eating,' or eating the liver of, her victim, or may cause her familiar "Bonga" to attack the unfortunate. That witches eat the liver is an old idea in India mentioned by the Mughal historians.

The Jan guru is employed to detect who is the woman responsible for any particular misfortune. His usual method is to gaze on a leaf smeared with oil, in which as in a crystal he can doubtless imagine that shapes present themselves. The witch having been detected, is liable to be beaten and maltreated until she withdraws her spells, and if this does not lead to the desired result she may be put to death.

Witchcraft.

The higher castes do not believe in witchcraft. If a man is ill they give him medicines and if he dies despite the medicine they do nothing further. But all the lower castes believe in witchcraft and know that it is a reality. The Santal women learned the craft first from Marang Burn by playing a trick on him when he meant to teach their husbands. And now they take quite little girls out by night and teach them so that the craft may not die out.

We know of many cases to prove that witchcraft is a reality. Perth who lives in Pankha's house was once ill: and it was an aunt of his who was "eating" him. One night as he lay ill the witch came and bent over him to take out his liver: but he woke up just in time and saw her and catching her by the hair he shouted for the people in the house. They and the villagers came and took the woman into custody. When the Pargana questioned her she confessed everything and was punished.

Another time a boy lay ill and senseless. A cowherd who was driving cattle home in the evening ran to the back of the house where the sick boy lay, after a cow which strayed there. There he found a woman in a state of possession (rum) he told the villagers what he had seen and they caught the woman and gave her a severe beating: whereupon the sick boy recovered. But about two months afterward the cowherd suddenly fell dead: and when they consulted a _jan_ as to the reason he said that it was the witch who had been beaten who had done it.

Ojha's and Dains.

Once upon a time, Marang Buru decided that he would teach men witchcraft. In those days there was a place at which men used to assemble to meet Marang Buru and hold council with him: but they only heard his voice and never saw his face. One day at the assembly when they had begun to tell Marang Buru of their troubles he fixed a day and told them to come to him on it, dressed all in their cleanest clothes and he would teach them witchcraft.

So the men all went home and told their wives to wash their clothes well against the fixed day, as they were going to Thakur to learn witchcraft. The women of course all began to discuss this new plan among themselves and the more they talked of it the less they liked it; it seemed to them that if the men were to get this new strange power it would make them more inclined to despise and bully women than ever; so they made a plot to get the better of their husbands. They arranged that each woman should brew some rice beer and offer it to her husband as he was starting to meet Marang Buru and beg him to drink some lest his return should be delayed. They foresaw that the men would not be able to resist the drink; and that had started they would go on till they were dead drunk: it would then be easy for the women to dress like men and go off to Marang Buru and learn witchcraft in place of their husbands. So said, so done;-- the women duly made their husbands drunk and then put on _pagris_ and _dhoties_ and stuck goats' beards on their faces and went off to Marang Buru to learn witchcraft. Marang Buru did not detect the imposition and according to his promise taught them all the incantations of witchcraft.

After the women had come home with their new knowledge their husbands gradually recovered their senses and bethought them of their appointment with Marang Buru. So they hurried off to the meeting place and asked him to teach them what he had promised. "Why I taught it all to you this morning," answered Marang Buru, "what do you mean by coming to me again?" The men could not understand what he meant and protested that they had not been to him at all in the morning. "Then you must have told your wives what I was going to do!" This they could not deny: "I see," said Marang Buru "then they must have played a trick on you and learned the _mantras_ in your place," At this, the men began to lament and begged that they might be taught also: but Marang Buru said that this was impossible; he could only teach them a very little; their wives had reaped the crop and they could only have the gleanings; so saying, he taught them the art of the _ojha_ and so that they might have the advantage of their wives in one respect and be able to overawe them he also taught them the craft of the _Jan_ and with that, they had to be content. This is why only women are witches.

Witchcraft initiation.

When girls are initiated into witchcraft they are taken away by force and made to lead tigers about. This makes them fearless. They are then taken to all the most powerful _bongas_ in succession; and are taught to invoke them, as school boys are taught lessons, and to become possessed _(rum)_. They are also taught _mantras_ and songs and by degree, they cease to be afraid. The novice is made to come out of the house with a lamp in her hand and a broom tied around her waist; she is then conducted to the great _bongas_ one of who approves of her and when all have agreed she is married to that _bonga_. The _bonga_ pays the usual bride price and applies _sindur_ to her forehead. After this, she can also marry a man in the usual way and he also pays the bride price. When a girl has learned everything she is made to take her degree (_sid atang_) by taking out a man's liver and cooking it with rice in a new pot; then she and the young woman who is initiating her, eat the feast together; a woman who has once eaten such a stew is completely proficient and can never forget what she has learned.

This is how girls learn witchcraft, and if any girl refuses to take the final step and will not eat men she is caused to go mad or die. Those however who have once eaten men have a craving for it.

Generally, it is only women who are witches, but some men have learned witchcraft and there are others who without being initiated have kept company with witches. For instance, in Simra village there is Chortha who was once a servant of the Parganas. He says that Parganna's wife used to take him out with her at night. The women used to sacrifice fowls and goats and make him skin them and cut them up: he had then to roast cakes of the flesh and give them to the Parganna's wife who distributed them among the other women.

Sometimes also witches take a man with them to their meetings to beat the drum: and sometimes if a man is very much in love with a girl he is allowed to go with them and is taught witchcraft. For instance, there was a man who had a family of daughters and no son and so he engaged a manservant by the year to work for him.

After being some years in service this manservant one night was for some reason unusually late in letting the buffaloes out to graze, and while doing so he saw all the women of the household assembled out of doors; they came up to him and told him not to be afraid and promised to do him no harm provided he told no one what he had seen. Two or three days later the young women of the house invited him to go to a witches' meeting. He went but felt rather frightened the whole time; however nothing happened to him, so he got over his fear and after that, he used to go with them quite willingly and learned all about witchcraft. At last, they told him that he must _sid atang_ by "eating" a human being. He objected that he was an orphan and so there was no relation with whom he could eat. This was a difficulty that seemed insurmountable, and he suggested that he should be excused the full course and taught only a little such as how to "eat" fowls. The women agreed but it was arranged that to deceive people he should go for two or three days and study with a _Jan guru_ and be initiated by him. Thus it would be thought that he learned his magic from the _guru_ but he learned it from the witches who taught him everything except how to "eat" human beings. He learned how to make trees wither away and come to life again, and to make rain fall where he wished while any place he chose remained quite dry; he learned to walk upon the surface of the water without getting wet; he could exorcise hail so that none would touch his house though it fell all around. For a joke, he could make stools stick fast to his friends when they sat on them, and anyone he scolded found himself unable to speak properly. All this we have seen him do, but it was no one's business to question him to find out how much he knew.

Once at the shield and sword dance they cast a spell on a youth till his clothes fell off him in shreds and he was ashamed to dance. Then this servant had the pieces of cloth brought to him, and he covered them with his cloth and mumbled some _mantras_ and blew on it and the pieces joined together and the cloth was as good as ever. This we have seen ourselves.

He lived a long time with his master who found him a wife; but because his first child died he left the place and went to live near Amrahat where he is now.

Another case is Tipu of Mohulpahari. They say that an old witch Dukkia taught him to be an _ojha_. No one has dared to ask him whether he also learned witchcraft from her but he admits that she taught him to be an _ojha_.

Although it is true that there are witches and that they "eat" men you will never see them except when you are alone.

The son-in-law of Surai of Karmatane village, named Khade, died from meeting witches; he told us all about it as he lay dying. He was coming home with some other men: they had all had a little too much to drink and so they got separated. Khade was coming along alone and had nearly reached his house when he saw a crowd of witches under a tree. He went up and asked who they were. Thereupon they turned on him and seized him and dragged him away towards Mancha. There they did something to him and let him go. The next morning he was seized with purging and by mistake, some of the witches' vengeance fell also on the other men and they were taken ill too. They however recovered, but Khade died. If you meet witches you die, but not of course if they take you with them of their own will and teach you their craft.

Witchcraft.

Girls are taught witchcraft when they are young and are married to a _bonga_ husbands. Afterward when they marry a man they still go away and visit the _bonga_ and when they do so they send in their place a _bonga_ woman exactly like them in appearance and voice; so that the husband cannot tell that it is not his real wife. There is however a way of discovering the substitution; for if the man takes a brand from the fire and burns the woman with it, then if it is a _bonga_ and not his wife she will fly away in a flame of fire.

TWO

I will now tell you something I have seen with my own eyes. In the village of Dhubia next to mine the only son of the Paranik lay ill for a whole year. One day I went out to look at my _rahar_ crop which was nearly ripe and as I stood under a mouth tree I heard a voice whispering. I stooped down to try and see through the _rahar_ who was there but the crop was so thick that I could see nothing; so I climbed up the mouth tree to look. Glancing towards Dhubia village I saw the third daughter of the Paranik come out of her house and walk towards me. When about fifty yards from me she climbed a big rock and waited. Presently an old aunt of hers came out of the village and joined her. Then the old woman went back to her house and returned with a lot of water. Meanwhile, the girl had come down from the rock and sat at its foot near a thicket of _dhela_ trees. The old woman caused the girl to become possessed (_rum_) and they had some conversation which I could not hear, Then they poured out the water from the lota and went home.

On my way home I met a young fellow from the village and found that he had also seen what the two women did. We went together to the place and found the mark of the water spilled on the ground and two leaves which had been used as wrappers and one of which was smeared with vermilion and _adwa_ rice had been scattered about. We decided to tell no one till we saw whether what had been done was meant to benefit or injure the sick boy. Fifteen days later the boy died: and when his parents consulted a _jan_ he named a young woman of the village as the cause of the boy's death and she was taken and punished severely by the villagers.

It is plain that the boy's sister and aunt to save themselves caused the _jan_ to see an innocent woman. I could not bring the boy back to life so it was useless for me to say anything, especially as the guilty women were of the Paranik's own family. This I saw myself in broad daylight.

It is plain that the boy's sister and aunt to save themselves caused the _jan_ to see an innocent woman. I could not bring the boy back to life so it was useless for me to say anything, especially as the guilty women were of the Paranik's own family. This I saw myself in broad daylight.

Another thing that happened to me was this. I had been with the Headman to pay the village rent. It was night when we returned and after leaving him I was going home alone. As I passed in front of a house a bright light suddenly shone from the cowshed; I looked around and saw a great crowd of women-witches standing there. I ran away by the garden at the back of the house until I reached a high road; then I stopped and looked around and saw that the witches were coming after me, and looked towards the hamlet where my house was as I saw that the witches were coming with bright light from that direction also. When I found myself thus hemmed in I felt that my last hour had come but I ran on till I came to some jungle.

Looking back from there I saw that the two bands had joined together and were coming after me. I did not feel safe there for I knew that there were _bongas_ in the jungle who might tell the witches where I was. So I ran on to the _tola_ where an uncle and aunt of mine lived. As I ran down the street I saw two witches at the back of one of the houses. They were sitting down; one was in a state of possession _(rum)_ and the other was opposite her holding a lamp. So I left the street and made my way through the fields till I Came to my uncle's house. I knocked and was admitted panting and breathless; my uncle and aunt went outside to see what it was that had scared me and they saw the witches with the two lights flashing and made haste to bolt the door. None of us slept for the rest of the night and in the morning I told them all that had happened.

Since that night I have been very frightened of witches and do not like to go out at night. It was lucky that the witches did not recognize me; otherwise, I should not have lived. Ever since I have never stayed at home for long together; I go there for two or three months at a time and then go away and work elsewhere. I am too frightened to stay in my village. Now all the old women who taught witchcraft are dead except one: when she goes I shall not be frightened anymore. I shall be able to go home when I like. I have never told anyone but my uncle and aunt what I saw until now that I have written it down.

So from my own experience, I do not doubt the existence of witches; I cannot say how they "eat" men, whether by magic or whether they order _"bongs"_ to cause a certain man to die on a certain day. Some people say that when a witch is first initiated she is married to a _bonga_ and if she wants to "eat" a man she orders her _bonga_ husband to kill him and if he refuses she heaps abuse on him until he does.

THREE

Young girls are taught witchcraft against their will and if they refuse to "eat" their father or brother they die or go mad. There was a girl in my village and she went out gathering herbs with another girl who was a witch. As usual, they sang at their work and the witch girl sang songs the tune of which the other thought so pretty that she learned them by heart. When she had learned them the witch girl told her that they were witch songs and explained to her their meaning. The girl was very angry at having been taught them unawares but the witch girl assured her that she would never be able to forget the songs or their interpretation; then she assigned her to a _bonga_ bridegroom and then told her to _sid atang_ and all would be well with her otherwise she would have trouble.

When the girl learned that she must _sid atang_ by "eating" her father or brother or mother she began to make excuses; she could not kill her father for he was the support of the family; nor her only brother for he was wanted too at the _Baha_ and _Sohrai_ nor her mother who had reared her in childhood. The witch girl said that if she refused she would die, and she said that she would rather die than do what was required of her. Then the witch did something and the girl began to rave and talk gibberish and from that time was quite out of her senses. _Ojhas_ tried to cure her in vain until at last one suggested that she should be taken to another village as the madness must be the work of witches living in her village. So they took her away and the remedies then cured her. She stayed in her new home and was married there. A long time afterward she went back to pay a visit to her father's house: but the day after she arrived her head began to ache and she fell ill and though her husband came and took her away she died the day after she reached her home.

When the girl learned that she must _sid atang_ by "eating" her father or brother or mother she began to make excuses; she could not kill her father for he was the support of the family; nor her only brother for he was wanted too at the _Baha_ and _Sohrai_ nor her mother who had reared her in childhood. The witch girl said that if she refused she would die, and she said that she would rather die than do what was required of her. Then the witch did something and the girl began to rave and talk gibberish and from that time was quite out of her senses. _Ojhas_ tried to cure her in vain until at last one suggested that she should be taken to another village as the madness must be the work of witches living in her village. So they took her away and the remedies then cured her. She stayed in her new home and was married there. A long time afterward she went back to pay a visit to her father's house: but the day after she arrived her head began to ache and she fell ill and though her husband came and took her away she died the day after she reached her home.

FOUR

In the village of Mohulpahari, there was a youth named Jerba. He was a servant to Bepin Teli of Tempa and often had to come home in the dark after his day's work. One night he was coming back very late and before he saw where he was, suddenly came upon a crowd of witches standing under a hollow mouth tree at the foot of the field that the dhobie has taken. Just as he caught sight of them they seized hold of him and flung him down and did something which he could not remember--for he lost his senses when they threw him down. When he came to himself he managed to struggle free and run off. The witches pursued but failed to overtake him and he reached his home in a state of terror. The witches however had not finished with him for two or three days after they caused him to fall from a tree and break his arm. Ojha's were called in but their medicines did him no good. The arm mortified and maggots formed and in a few days Jerba himself told them that he would not recover; he told them how the witches chased him and that he had recognized them as women of his village and shortly afterward he became speechless and died.

My brother-in-law lived in Mubundi. One night he and several other men were sitting up on the threshing floor watching their rice. In the middle of the night, they saw lights shining and flickering in the courtyard of my brother-in-law's house and he went to see what was the matter. When he got near, the lights went into the house: he went up quietly, and as he looked in founding the house full of women who extinguished the light directly they saw him and rushed out of the house. Then he asked my sister what the light was; but she could only stammer out "What light? I saw no light," so he struck her a blow and went back to the threshing floor and told the others what he had seen. That night he would not tell them the names of the women he had seen, and before morning his right arm swelled and became very painful; the swelling quickly increased and by noon he lost consciousness, and a few hours later he died.

FIVE

Two Witches.

There were once a woman and her daughter-in-law who were both witches. One night during the annual Sohrai festival the men of the village were going from house to house singing and getting rice beer to drink; and one young man named Chandra got so drunk that when they came to the house where the two witch-women lived he rolled himself under the shelf on which rice was stored and fell asleep. The next morning he came to his senses but he did not like to come out and show himself for fear of ridicule so he made up his mind to wait till a party came round singing again and then to slip out with them unperceived.

He lay waiting and presently all the men of the house went away to join in the _danka_ dance; leaving the mistress of the house and her daughter-in-law alone. Presently, the two began to talk and the elder woman said: "Well what with the pigs and the goats that have been sacrificed during this Sohrai we have had plenty of meat to eat lately, and yet I don't feel as if I had had any." "That is so," answered her daughter-in-law; "fowls' and pig's flesh is very unsatisfying." "Then what are we to do?" rejoined the old woman, "I don't know unless you do for the father of your grandchild." When he heard this Chandra shivered with fright and hid further under the ice shelf, for he saw that the two women must be witches.

That day was the day on which a bullock is tied to a post outside each house and at noon the husband of the younger witch began to dig a hole outside the house to receive the post. While he was working Chandra heard the two women begin to talk again. "Now is your opportunity," said the younger woman, "while he is digging the hole." "But perhaps the _ojha_ will be able to discover us," objected the other. "Oh we can prevent that by making the _ojha_ see in the oiled leaf the faces of Rupi and Bindi--naming two girls of the village--and we can say that my husband had seduced them and then declined to marry them and that that was why they killed him." The old woman seemed to be satisfied, for she took up a hatchet and went out to where her son was digging the hole. She waited till he bent down to throw out the earth with his hands and then cut open his back and pulled out his liver and heart and brought them into the house. Her unfortunate son felt a spasm of pain when his mother struck him but he did not know what had hurt him and there was no visible wound. The two women then chopped up the liver and heart and cooked and ate them.

That night when the village youths came round to the house, singing, Chandra slipped out with them unperceived and hastened home. Two or three days later the bewitched man became seriously ill; medicines and sacrifices did him no good; the _ojhas_ was called in but could make nothing of the illness. The villagers were very angry with them for the failure and the headman told them that they must ascertain using the oiled leaf who had caused the illness, or it would be the worse for them. So the _ojhas_ went through their ceremonies and after a time declared that the oiled leaf showed the faces of the two girls Rupi and Bindi; and that it was they who were eating up the sick man. So the two girls were sent for and questioned but they solemnly swore that they knew nothing about the matter. No one believed their protestations and the headman ordered that filth should be put into their mouths and that they should be well beaten to make them confess. However before any harm was done to them Chandra sprang up and called out to the headman: "You have proof that these girls are witches, but I will not let you beat them here. Let us take them to yonder open field; the token of their oath is there and we will make them first remove it. If we beat them first they will probably refuse to remove the oath." "How do you know about their oath?" asked the headman. "Never mind, I do know." The villagers were convinced by his confident manner and all went with the two girls to the open field.

Chandra's object was to get away from the witches' house for he was afraid to speak there; but when they were out in the open he stood up and told the villagers all that he had seen and heard the two witches do; they remembered that he had been missing for a whole day during the Sohrai festival and believed him. So the sick man's wife and mother were fetched and well beaten to make them restore the sick man to health, but his liver and heart had been eaten so that the case was hopeless and in a few days he was dead. His relations in revenge soon killed the two witches.

Rupi and Bindi whose lives had been saved by Chandra went and established themselves in his house, for they declared that as they owed their lives to him it was plain that he must marry them.

SIX

The Lawful Wife's Witchy Sister.

There were once two brothers who lived together; the elder was married but the younger had no wife. The elder brother used to cultivate their lands and his wife used to draw water and fetch fuel and the younger brother used to take the cattle out to graze. One year when the elder brother was busy in the fields the younger one used to take his cattle to graze near where his brother was working and the wife used to bring out breakfast for both of them. One day the younger brother thought he would play a trick on his sister-in-law by not answering when she called him to his breakfast, so when her husband had finished his meal and she called out for the younger brother to come he gave no answer; she concluded that the cattle were straying and would not let him come so she took up her basket and went to look for him, but when he saw her coming he climbed up a tree and hid and for all her calling gave no answer, but only sat and laughed at her although she came quite close to where he was.

At last, the woman got into a passion and putting down the breakfast by the side of a pool which was close to the tree up which her brother-in-law had climbed she stripped off her clothes and began bowing down and calling. "Ho, Dharma Chandi! come forth!" When he saw this the man was amazed and waited to see whom she was calling, meaning to let her know he was there directly she turned to go away home with the breakfast. But the woman kept on calling to Dharmal Chandi and at last out of the pool appeared an immense bearded _bonga_ with long and matted hair. When the woman saw him her tongue flickered in and out like a snake's and she made a hissing noise, such as a crab makes. Then the woman began "Dharmal Chandi I have a request which you must promise to grant." And when the _bonga_ had promised she proceeded. "You must have my brother-in-law killed by a tiger the day after tomorrow; he has put me to endless trouble making me go shouting after him all through the jungle; I wanted to go back quickly because I have a lot of work at home; he has wasted my time by not answering; so the day after to-morrow you must have him killed." The _bonga_ promised to do what she asked and disappeared into the pool and the woman went home.

While the younger brother was up in the tree his cattle had got into a _gundli_ field and eaten up the crop: and the owner found it out and got the brothers fined. So that evening the elder brother asked him where he had been that he had not looked after the cattle properly nor eaten any breakfast. In answer the younger brother only began to cry; at that his sister-in-law said. "Let him alone; he is crying for want of a wife; he is going silly because we have not married him;" and so nothing more was said. But the elder brother was not satisfied and the next day when they went together to work he asked the younger what was the real reason for his crying.

Then the younger answered. "Brother, I am in great trouble; it makes me cry all day; if you wish ever to look on my face again, you must not work in the fields tomorrow but keep me company while I tend the cattle; if we are separated for a moment a tiger will kill me; it will be quickly over for me but you I know will miss me much and so I am grieving for you; if you have any tenderness for me do not leave me to-morrow but save me from the tiger." His brother asked the reason for this foreboding but the younger man said that he would explain nothing and accuse no one until the events of the next day had shown whether he was speaking the truth; if a tiger came to stalk him then that would be proof that he had had good reason for his apprehension, and he begged his brother not to speak a word about it to anyone and especially not to his wife.

The elder brother promised to keep the matter a secret and cheered his brother up and told him to be of good heart; they would take their bows and axes and he would like to see the tiger that would touch them. So the next morning the two brothers went off together well armed and tended the cattle in the company; nothing happened and at midday, they brought the cattle home; when the woman saw them with bows in their hands she asked where they had been. Her husband told her that he had been to look for a hare which he had seen on the previous day but he had not been able to find it. Then his brother said that he had seen a hare in its form that very morning but had not had time to shoot it. So they pretended to arrange to go and hunt this hare and after having eaten their rice they drove out the cattle again.

As they went along they kept close together with their arrows on the string, so that the tiger which came to stalk the younger brother got no opportunity to attack; at last, it showed itself at the edge of the jungle; the cattle were thrown into a turmoil and the brothers saw that it was following them, and the elder brother was convinced that there was some reason for his brother's fears. So they turned the cattle back and cautiously drove them home, keeping a good lookout all the way; the tiger prowled around them hiding in the bushes, sometimes in front and sometimes behind, but found no opening to attack while they for their part did not dare to shoot at it. The tiger followed them right up to the house, but the elder brother did not leave the other for a moment nor let him go outside the door and at night he slept on the same bed with him.

The next morning he begged his brother to tell him all that had happened and explain how he knew that a tiger would seek his life on the previous day. "Come then," said the other, "to yonder open ground. I cannot tell you in the house;" so they went out together and then the younger told all that had happened and how his sister-in-law had ordered the _Bonga_ to have him killed by a tiger; "I did not tell you before till my story had been put to the proof for fear that you would not believe me and would tell your wife, but now you know all. I cannot live with you any longer; from this very day I must go and find a home elsewhere." "Not so," said the other, "I will not keep such a woman with me any longer; she is dangerous; I will go home now and put her to death," and so saying he went home and killed his wife with an ax.

SEVEN

BONGA RAMJIT.

Once upon a time, a man went out to snare quail: he set his snares by the side of a mountain stream and then sat down under a bush to watch them. As he waited he saw a young woman come along with her water pot under her arm to draw water from the stream. When she got to the _ghat_ she put down her pot and made her way up the stream towards where the snares had been set; she did not notice the hunter but went to the stump of an ebony tree near him and looked around and seeing no one she suddenly became possessed and started dancing around the ebony tree and singing some song which he could not catch; and as she danced she called out "The Pig's fat is overflowing: brother-in-law Ramjit come here to me." When she called out like this the quail catcher quietly crept nearer still to her. Although the woman repeatedly summoned him in this way the Bonga would not come out because he was aware of the presence of the onlooker; the woman however got into passion at his non-appearance and stripping off her clothes she danced naked around the tree calling out "The Pig's fat is overflowing: brother-in-law Ramjit come hither at once." At last out of the _nala_ appeared the Bonga, dark, enormous, and shaggy; and approached the woman: Then the woman said "Brother-in-law Ramjit there is something that you must do for me; my nephew is ill; he must die on such and such a day; that day I must see the smoke of his funeral pyre; but you must save me from the witch-finder; let the blame fall not on me but on so and so; this is what I came to urge on you; that you protect me from discovery and then we shall always be friends."

The Bonga at first knowing that they were being watched would not make the promise but when the woman insisted he promised in a low voice and then disappeared into the _nala_; and the witch went back to the ghat, filled her water pot, and went home. The quail catcher also went trembling home and he remembered the day fixed for the death of the nephew of the witch and he decided to wait and see what happened before saying anything to the villagers. Sure enough on the day before that fixed by the witch, the invalid became unconscious and was obviously at the point of death. When he heard this the quail catcher went to the sick man's bedside and seeing his condition told his relatives to collect all the villagers to beat the woman whom he had seen with the Bonga and he told them all that had passed; the villagers believed him and summoning all the women of the village they scolded them, and then being excited by this they rose and began to beat the women; to each, they gave one blow with a stick, but the woman whom the quail catcher pointed out they beat till she fainted.

Then they ordered her to cure the sick man and threatened to burn her along with him if he died, but she insisted that she was innocent. Then they told her that they knew all that had passed between her and the Bonga Ramjit, she persisted that it was all a mistake. So they started to beat her again; they beat her from her heels to her neck and then from her neck down to her heels till the blood flowed and they swore that they would not let her go unless she cured the sick man and that if he died they would cut her to pieces. At last, the torture made her confess that it was she who was eating the sick man, and she promised to cure him; so they first made her tell the names of all the other witches in the village and then tied her to a post and kept her there and did not untie her till in four or five days the sick man recovered. When she was let loose the quail catcher ran away from the village and would not live there anymore.

But the villagers threatened the witch woman that if her nephew or any of his family got ill again they would kill her, and they told her that as her secret had been found out she was henceforth to be their _ojha_ and cure their diseases; and they would supply her with whatever she wanted for the purpose; they asked what sacrifice her nephew must make on his recovery; and she told them to get a red cock, a grasshopper: a lizard; a cat and a black and white goat; so they brought her these and she sacrificed them and the villagers had a feast of rice and rice beer and went to their homes and the matter ended.

EIGHT

THE WITCHES AND THE HERD BOY.

Once upon a time a cowherd lost a calf and while looking for it he was benighted in the jungle; for he was afraid to go home lest he should be scolded for losing the calf. He had with him his bow and arrows and flute and a stick but still, he was afraid to stay the night in the jungle; so he made up his mind to go to the _jahirthan_ as _More Turuiko_ would protect him there; so he went to the _jahir than_ and climbed a tree in which a spirit abode; he took his bow and arrows up with him but he was too frightened to go to sleep.

About supper time he saw several women who were witches collect from all sides at the _jahir than_: at this sight,, he was more frightened than ever; the witches then called up the _bongas_ and they also summoned two tigers; then they danced the _lagre_ dance and they combed the hair of the two tigers. Then they also called _More Turniko_ and when they came, one Bonga said "I smell a man" and

More Turniko scolded him saying "Faith, you smelt nothing until we came; and directly we come you say you smell a man; it must be us your smell"; and the chief of the _bongas_ agreed that it must be all right. Then while the women were dancing the boy took his bow and shot the two tigers, and the tigers enraged by their wounds fell on the witches and killed them all, and then they died themselves, and as they were dying they roared terribly so that the people in the villages near heard them. When it grew light the boy climbed down and drawing the arrows from the bodies of the tigers went home.

Then the people asked him where he had spent the night and he said that he was benighted while looking for his calf and as he heard tigers roaring near the _jahir than_ he was frightened and had stayed in the jungle. They told him that when the tigers began to roar the calf had come running home by itself and this was good news to the herd boy. Then he found that all the children in the village were crying for their mothers and the men were asking what had become of their wives; then the herdboy said that in the night he had seen some women going in the direction of the _jahir than_ but he had not seen them come back and they had better go and look there. So the villagers went off and found their wives lying dead by the _jahir than_ and the two tigers also dead, and they knew that the women must have been witches to go there at night; so they wept over them and burned the bodies. And a long time afterward the boy told them all that he had seen and done; and they admitted that he had done right in destroying the witches and that it would be well if all witches met the same fate.

This story whether true or not is told to this day.

NINE

A MAN-TIGER

There was once a young man who when a boy had learned witchcraft from some girlfriends; was married but his wife knew nothing about this. They lived happily together and were in the habit of paying frequent visits to the wife's parents. One day they were on their way together to pay such a visit and in passing through some jungle they saw, grazing with a herd of cattle, a very fine and fat bull calf. The man stopped and stripped himself to his waist cloth and told his wife to hold his clothes for him while he went and ate the calf that had stirred his appetite. His wife in astonishment asked him how he was going to eat a living animal; he answered that he was going to turn into a tiger and kill the animal and he impressed on her that she must on no account be frightened or run away and he handed her a piece of root and told her that she must give it to him to smell when he came back and he would at once regain his human shape.

So saying he retired into a thicket and took off his waist cloth and at once became a tiger; then he swallowed the waist cloth and thereby grew a fine long tail. Then he sprang upon the calf and knocked it over and began to suck its blood. At this sight, his wife was overwhelmed with terror and forgetting everything in her fear ran right off to her father's house taking with her her husband's clothes and the magic root. She arrived breathlessly and told her parents all that had happened. Meanwhile, her husband had been deprived of the means of regaining his form and was forced to spend the day hiding in the jungle as a tiger; when night fell he made his way to the village where his father-in-law lived. But when he got there all the dogs began to bark and when the villagers saw that there was a tiger they barricaded themselves in their houses.

The man-tiger went prowling around his father-in-law's house and at last, his father-in-law plucked up courage and went out and threw the root which the wife had brought under the tiger's nose and he at once became a man again. Then they brought him into the house and washed his feet; and gave him hot rice water to drink, and on drinking this he vomited up lumps of clotted blood. The next morning the father-in-law called the villagers and showed them this blood and told them all that had happened; then he turned to his son-in-law and told him to take himself off and vowed that his daughter should never go near him again. The man-tiger had no answer to make but went back silently and alone to his own home.

_Note:— The recipe for creating a were-tiger or Plant bag is as follows.

"Bauhinia vali fiber, hammered out and fried in mustard oil in a human skull."

9 798887 721866

Printed by Libri Plureos GmbH in Hamburg,
Germany